THE
INVISIBLE MAN

H. G. WELLS

COACH & HORSES INN

THE STRANGER CAME TO IPING VILLAGE IN ENGLAND ON THE NINTH DAY OF FEBRUARY, THROUGH A BITING WIND AND DRIVING SNOW, CARRYING A LITTLE BLACK PORTMANTEAU IN HIS THICKLY GLOVED HAND.
HE WAS WRAPPED UP FROM HEAD TO FOOT, AND THE BRIM OF HIS SOFT FELT HAT HID EVERY INCH OF HIS FACE.

HE STAGGERED INTO THE COACH AND HORSES INN MORE DEAD THAN ALIVE.

I MUST HAVE A ROOM AND A FIRE!

OF COURSE, SIR.

THE PROPRIETESS OF THE INN, MRS HALL, LED THE WAY TO A ROOM.

MAY I TAKE YOUR COAT AND HAT, SIR, AND GIVE THEM A GOOD DRY IN THE KITCHEN?

NO!

VERY WELL, SIR. THE ROOM WILL BE WARMER SOON.

WHEN SHE RETURNED, THE MAN WAS STILL STANDING WHERE SHE HAD LEFT HIM.

YOUR LUNCH, SIR.

ONLY THEN DID THE STRANGER TURN AROUND. MRS HALL STOOD GAPING AT HIM, FOR HIS HEAD WAS COMPLETELY MUFFLED IN BANDAGES.

AH, I DIDN'T KNOW, SIR. YOU'VE HAD AN ACCIDENT?

YES, I CAME TO IPING HOPING TO BE ABLE TO LIVE AND WORK HERE WITHOUT BEING DISTURBED. I AM AN EXPERIMENTAL INVESTIGATOR.

OH YES, SIR, AND IF I MAY MAKE SO BOLD AS TO ASK...

THAT WILL BE ALL, MRS HALL.

THE FOLLOWING DAY, THE STRANGER'S BAGGAGE ARRIVED.

COME ALONG WITH THOSE BOXES. I'VE BEEN WAITING LONG ENOUGH.

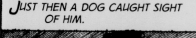

JUST THEN A DOG CAUGHT SIGHT OF HIM.

GROWLING SAVAGELY, HE LEAPT AT THE STRANGER AND FASTENED HIS TEETH IN HIS LEG.

THE STRANGER'S TROUSER LEG TORE. HE TURNED AND RUSHED BACK INTO THE INN.

IT'S A FUNNY THING. I LOOKED THROUGH THE TEAR IN HIS TROUSERS, AND I DIDN'T SEE ANYTHING. THERE WAS NOTHING THERE!

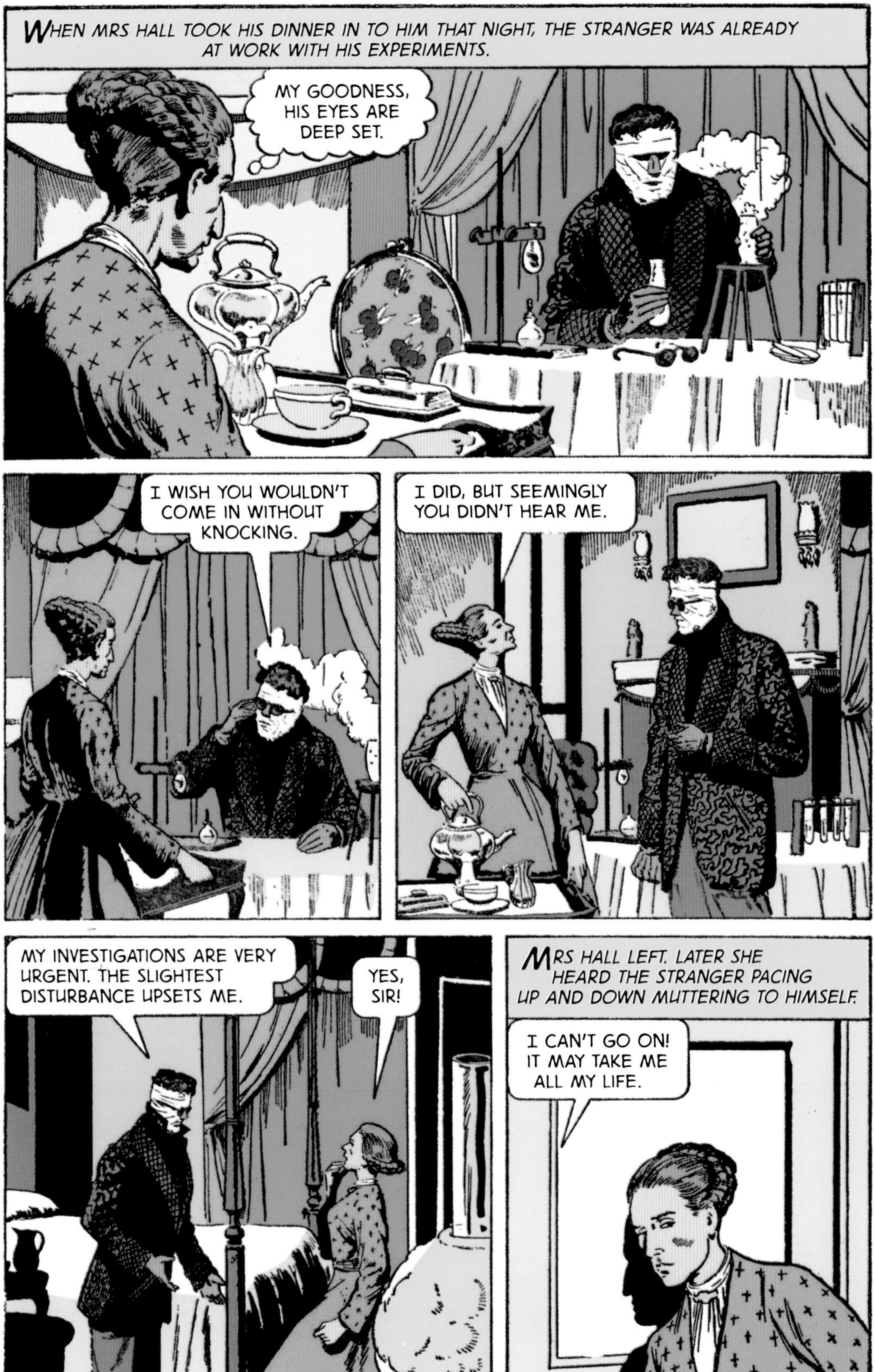
WHEN MRS HALL TOOK HIS DINNER IN TO HIM THAT NIGHT, THE STRANGER WAS ALREADY AT WORK WITH HIS EXPERIMENTS.
MY GOODNESS, HIS EYES ARE DEEP SET.
I WISH YOU WOULDN'T COME IN WITHOUT KNOCKING.
I DID, BUT SEEMINGLY YOU DIDN'T HEAR ME.
MY INVESTIGATIONS ARE VERY URGENT. THE SLIGHTEST DISTURBANCE UPSETS ME.
YES, SIR!
MRS HALL LEFT. LATER SHE HEARD THE STRANGER PACING UP AND DOWN MUTTERING TO HIMSELF.
I CAN'T GO ON! IT MAY TAKE ME ALL MY LIFE.

THE STRANGER CONTINUED HIS EXPERIMENTS FOR SEVERAL MONTHS. ONE DAY THE LOCAL DOCTOR, DEVOURED BY CURIOSITY, CALLED ON HIM.

PARDON MY INTRUSION, BUT I SEE YOU ARE DOING RESEARCH.

YES.

IS IT MEDICAL BY CHANCE?

BLAST YOU! WHAT ARE YOU FISHING FOR?

THE STRANGER GESTURED, AND HIS HAND CAME OUT OF HIS POCKET.

LORD! HE'S GOT NO ARM!

HOW THE DEVIL CAN YOU MOVE AN EMPTY SLEEVE LIKE THAT?

YOU SAW AN EMPTY SLEEVE?

CERTAINLY.

SLOWLY THE STRANGER EXTENDED THE SLEEVE TOWARD THE DOCTOR.

WHEN IT WAS SIX INCHES AWAY, HE STOPPED.

THERE'S NOTHING THERE!

THEN SOMETHING NIPPED THE DOCTOR'S NOSE.

HE TURNED AND FLED

IT FELT LIKE A THUMB AND FINGER, BUT THERE WAS NOTHING THERE.

SEVERAL DAYS LATER, THERE WAS A BURGLARY AT THE VICARAGE. IT WAS JUST BEFORE DAWN AND THE VICAR, MR BUNTING, AND HIS WIFE WERE ASLEEP.

SUDDENLY MRS BUNTING AWOKE.

I THINK SOMEONE IS WALKING AROUND DOWNSTAIRS!

THE VICAR ARMED HIMSELF WITH A POKER. THEN THEY DESCENDED THE STAIRCASE AS NOISELESSLY AS POSSIBLE.

SEE, SOMEONE HAS LIT A CANDLE IN THE STUDY.

GRIPPING THE POKER FIRMLY, THE VICAR RUSHED IN.

SURRENDER!

THE ROOM WAS PERFECTLY EMPTY.

BUT LOOK, THE HOUSEKEEPING MONEY IS GONE!

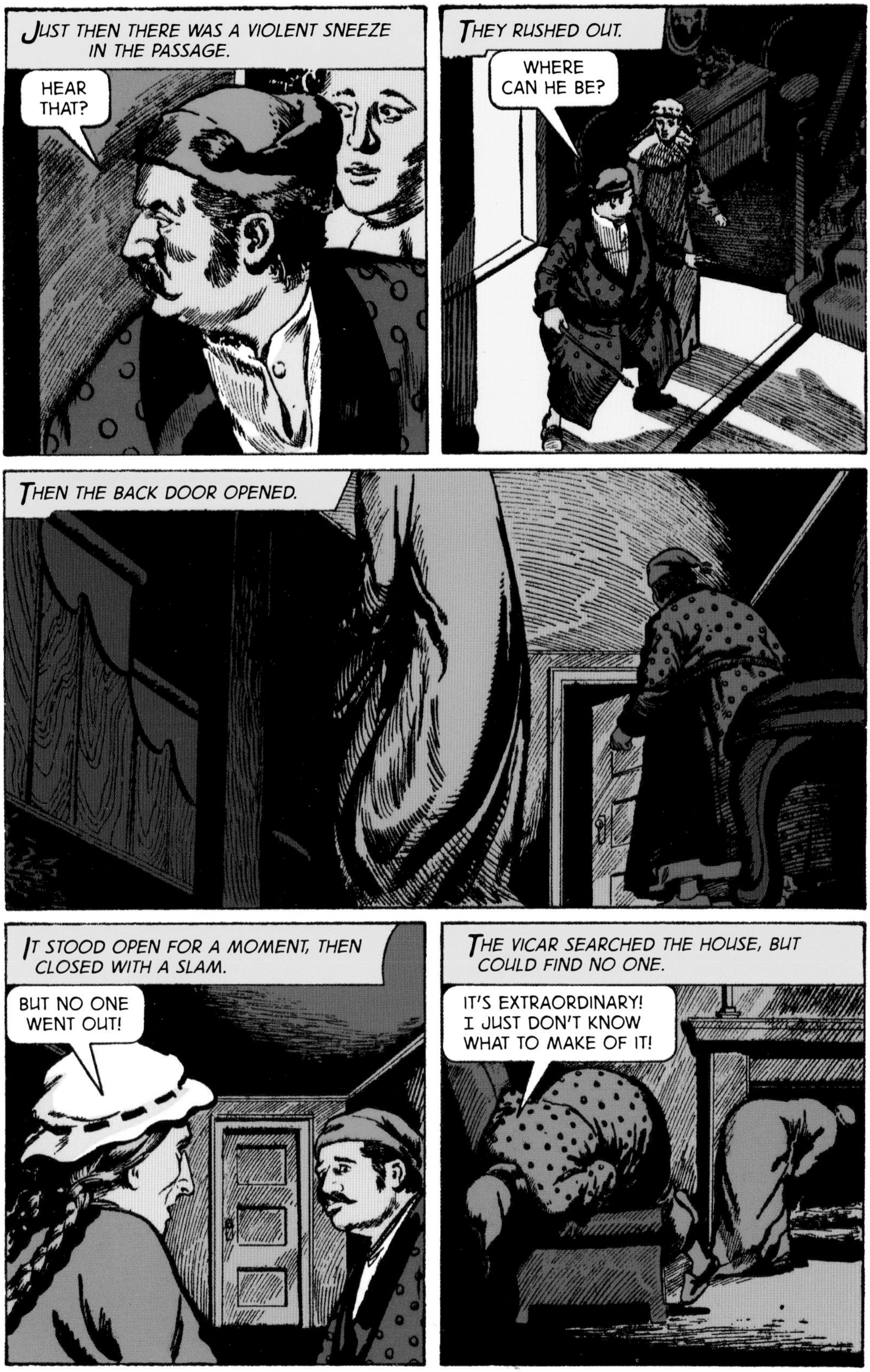
JUST THEN THERE WAS A VIOLENT SNEEZE IN THE PASSAGE.
HEAR THAT?
THEY RUSHED OUT.
WHERE CAN HE BE?
THEN THE BACK DOOR OPENED.
IT STOOD OPEN FOR A MOMENT, THEN CLOSED WITH A SLAM.
BUT NO ONE WENT OUT!
THE VICAR SEARCHED THE HOUSE, BUT COULD FIND NO ONE.
IT'S EXTRAORDINARY! I JUST DON'T KNOW WHAT TO MAKE OF IT!

MRS HALL WAS UP VERY EARLY THAT SAME MORNING.

THAT'S ODD. I KNOW I BOLTED THE FRONT DOOR LAST NIGHT.

THEN SHE PASSED BY THE STRANGER'S ROOM AND SAW HIS DOOR WAS AJAR.

SHE PUSHED IT OPEN AND ENTERED.

HE'S GONE, BUT HE'S LEFT HIS CLOTHES. THIS IS A CURIOUS BUSINESS.

SHE FANCIED SHE HEARD THE FRONT DOOR OPEN AND SHUT. THEN SHE THOUGHT SHE HEARD A SNIFF BEHIND HER.

SUDDENLY, THE BEDCLOTHES LEAPT UP INTO A SORT OF PEAK.

IMMEDIATELY AFTER, THE STRANGER'S HAT DASHED STRAIGHT AT HER FACE.

THEN THE CHAIR TURNED ITSELF UP AND CHARGED AT HER.

SHE SCREAMED AND TURNED, AND THE CHAIR LEGS IMPELLED HER OUT OF THE ROOM.

THE DOOR SLAMMED VIOLENTLY BEHIND HER.

IT'S SPIRITS! THAT MAN'S PUT SPIRITS IN MY FURNITURE!

MRS HALL WATCHED FOR THE STRANGER'S RETURN UNTIL NEARLY MID-DAY. THEN, STRANGELY, HE CAME DOWN THE STAIRS FROM HIS ROOM.

MRS HALL! WHY WASN'T MY BREAKFAST LAID?

I THOUGHT YOU WERE OUT HOW DID YOU GET IN AGAIN?

THOSE AS STOPS IN THIS HOUSE COMES IN BY THE DOORS, AND THAT YOU DIDN'T DO. AND I WANT TO KNOW...

STOP!

YOU DON'T UNDERSTAND WHO I AM, OR WHAT I AM. BY HEAVEN, I'LL SHOW YOU!

HE PUT HIS GLOVED HAND OVER HIS FACE AND WITHDREW IT. THE CENTRE BECAME A BLACK CAVITY.

THEN HE REMOVED HIS SPECTACLES AND HIS HAT.

WITH A VIOLENT GESTURE HE TORE AT HIS BANDAGES, AND OFF THEY CAME.

HE STOOD THERE – A SOLID FIGURE UP TO THE COAT COLLAR, AND THEN, NOTHING AT ALL.

THE PEOPLE AT THE INN RAN INTO THE STREET, SHOUTING AND SHRIEKING.

HELP! HELP! GET THE CONSTABLE!

THE CONSTABLE SOON ARRIVED.

HEAD OR NO HEAD, I'M GOING TO ARREST HIM.

THE CONSTABLE MARCHED INTO THE INN AND UP TO THE HEADLESS FIGURE.

OFF CAME THE STRANGER'S GLOVES.

KEEP AWAY!

SOMETHING STRUCK THE CONSTABLE IN THE FACE. HE MADE A GRAB FOR THE STRANGER.

He CAUGHT AT AN INVISIBLE THROAT BUT THE STRANGER PULLED AWAY.

Quickly HE FUMBLED WITH HIS CLOTHES.

WHY, THAT'S NOT A MAN AT ALL! IT'S JUST EMPTY CLOTHES.

THE FACT IS, I AM A MAN. BUT I'M INVISIBLE.

HE'S GOT HIS CLOTHES OFF. NOW WE'LL NEVER FIND HIM.

As EVERYONE SHOUTED AND FENCED THE AIR, THE DOOR OPENED AND THE INVISIBLE MAN WAS GONE.

LATER THAT DAY, A TRAMP NAMED MARVEL WAS SITTING BY A ROADSIDE A MILE AND A HALF OUT OF IPING WHEN HE HEARD A VOICE BEHIND HIM...

YOU, THERE!

WHO IS IT? WHERE ARE YOU?

HERE, NOW KEEP YOUR NERVES STEADY.

I MUST BE OFF MY BLOOMING CHUMP. I COULD HAVE SWORN I HEARD A VOICE.

OF COURSE YOU DID! I'M HERE, BUT I'M INVISIBLE. YOU'RE LOOKING THROUGH ME RIGHT NOW.

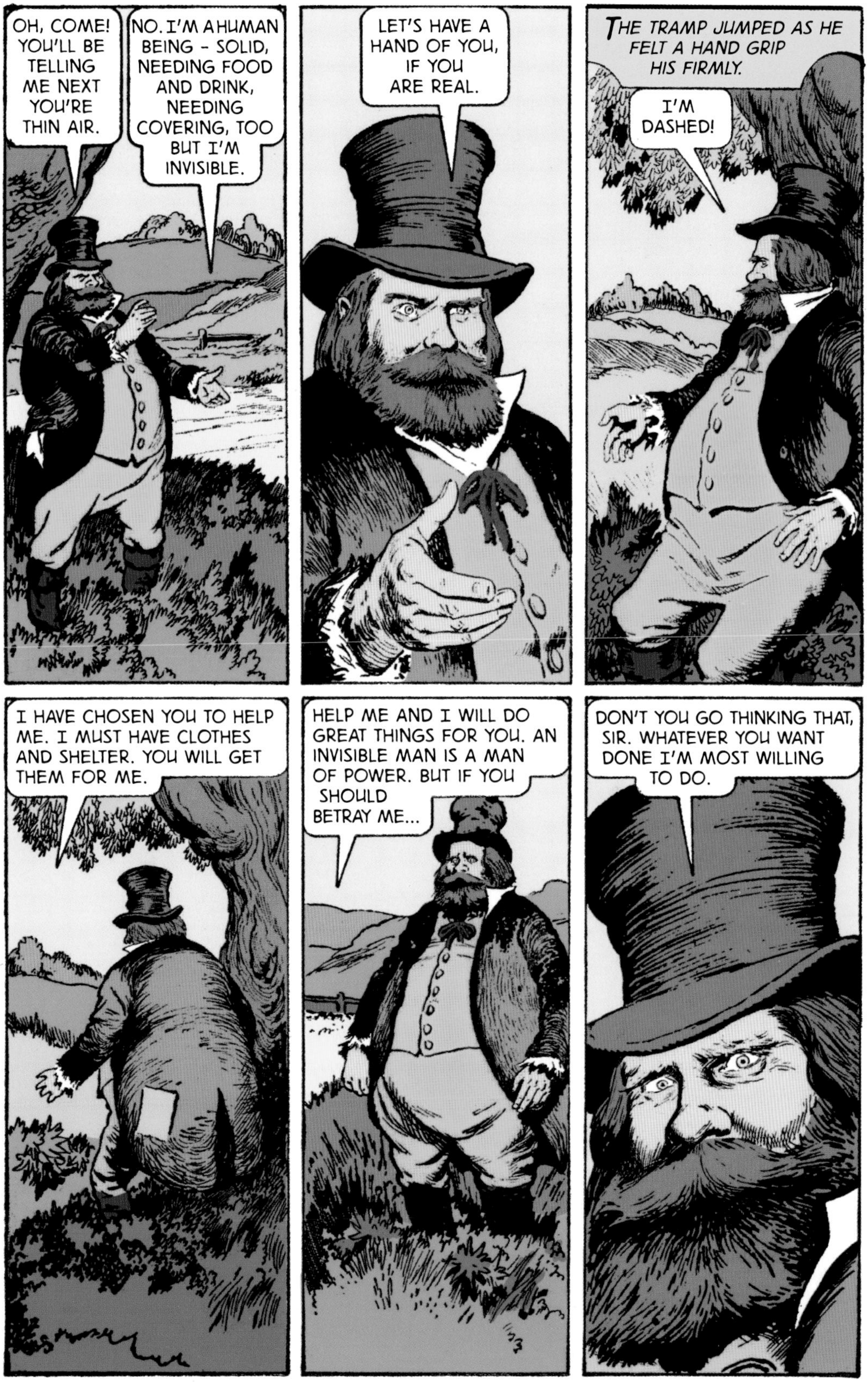
OH, COME! YOU'LL BE TELLING ME NEXT YOU'RE THIN AIR.
NO. I'M A HUMAN BEING - SOLID, NEEDING FOOD AND DRINK, NEEDING COVERING, TOO BUT I'M INVISIBLE.
LET'S HAVE A HAND OF YOU, IF YOU ARE REAL.
THE TRAMP JUMPED AS HE FELT A HAND GRIP HIS FIRMLY.
I'M DASHED!
I HAVE CHOSEN YOU TO HELP ME. I MUST HAVE CLOTHES AND SHELTER. YOU WILL GET THEM FOR ME.
HELP ME AND I WILL DO GREAT THINGS FOR YOU. AN INVISIBLE MAN IS A MAN OF POWER. BUT IF YOU SHOULD BETRAY ME...
DON'T YOU GO THINKING THAT, SIR. WHATEVER YOU WANT DONE I'M MOST WILLING TO DO.

FOR TWO DAYS MARVEL WAS FORCED TO HELP HIS INVISIBLE MASTER. THEN HE MANAGED TO SLIP AWAY. HE FLED IN TERROR TOWARDS THE VILLAGE OF PORT BURDOCK.

AS HE RAN, A DOG PLAYING IN THE ROAD BEHIND HIM YELPED AS IF KICKED. PEOPLE STROLLING HOMEWARD WERE JOSTLED BY AN UNSEEN FORCE.

AS THEY WONDERED WHAT IT WAS, SOMETHING - A WIND - A PAD, PAD, PAD - A SOUND LIKE A PANTING BREATHING, RUSHED BY.

MARVEL RAN INTO AN INN.

HE'S COMING! HE'S AFTER ME! FOR GOD'S SAKE, HIDE ME!

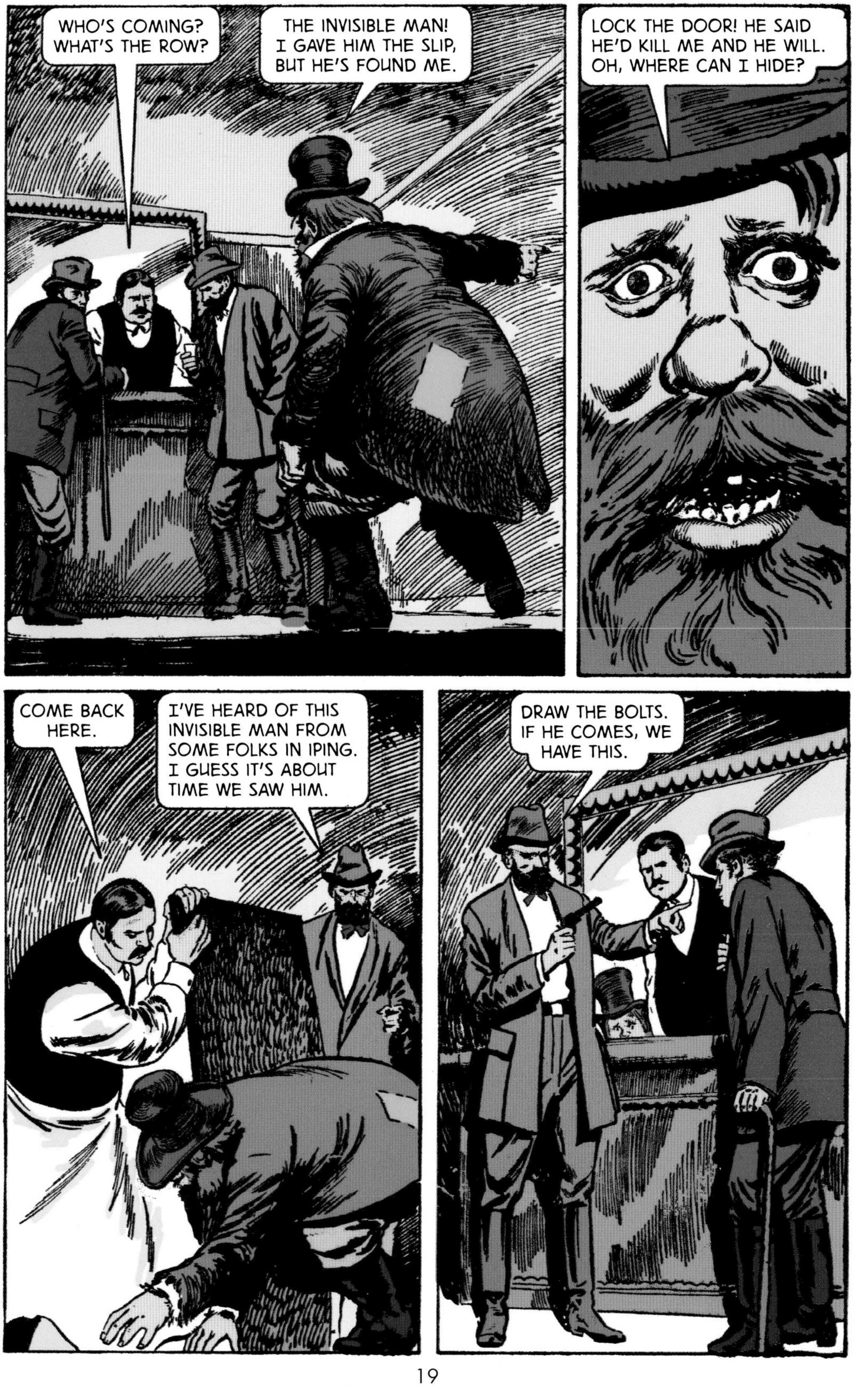
WHO'S COMING? WHAT'S THE ROW?
THE INVISIBLE MAN! I GAVE HIM THE SLIP, BUT HE'S FOUND ME.
LOCK THE DOOR! HE SAID HE'D KILL ME AND HE WILL. OH, WHERE CAN I HIDE?
COME BACK HERE.
I'VE HEARD OF THIS INVISIBLE MAN FROM SOME FOLKS IN IPING. I GUESS IT'S ABOUT TIME WE SAW HIM.
DRAW THE BOLTS. IF HE COMES, WE HAVE THIS.

THEY WAITED TENSELY, BUT THE DOOR REMAINED CLOSED.

ARE ALL THE OTHER DOORS LOCKED? HE'S PROWLING AROUND.

THERE'S THE BACK! I'LL SEE TO IT.

IN A MINUTE HE REAPPEARED.

THE YARD DOOR WAS OPEN.

HE MAY BE IN THE HOUSE RIGHT NOW!

HE'S NOT IN THE KITCHEN. I'VE STABBED EVERY INCH OF IT WITH THIS KNIFE.

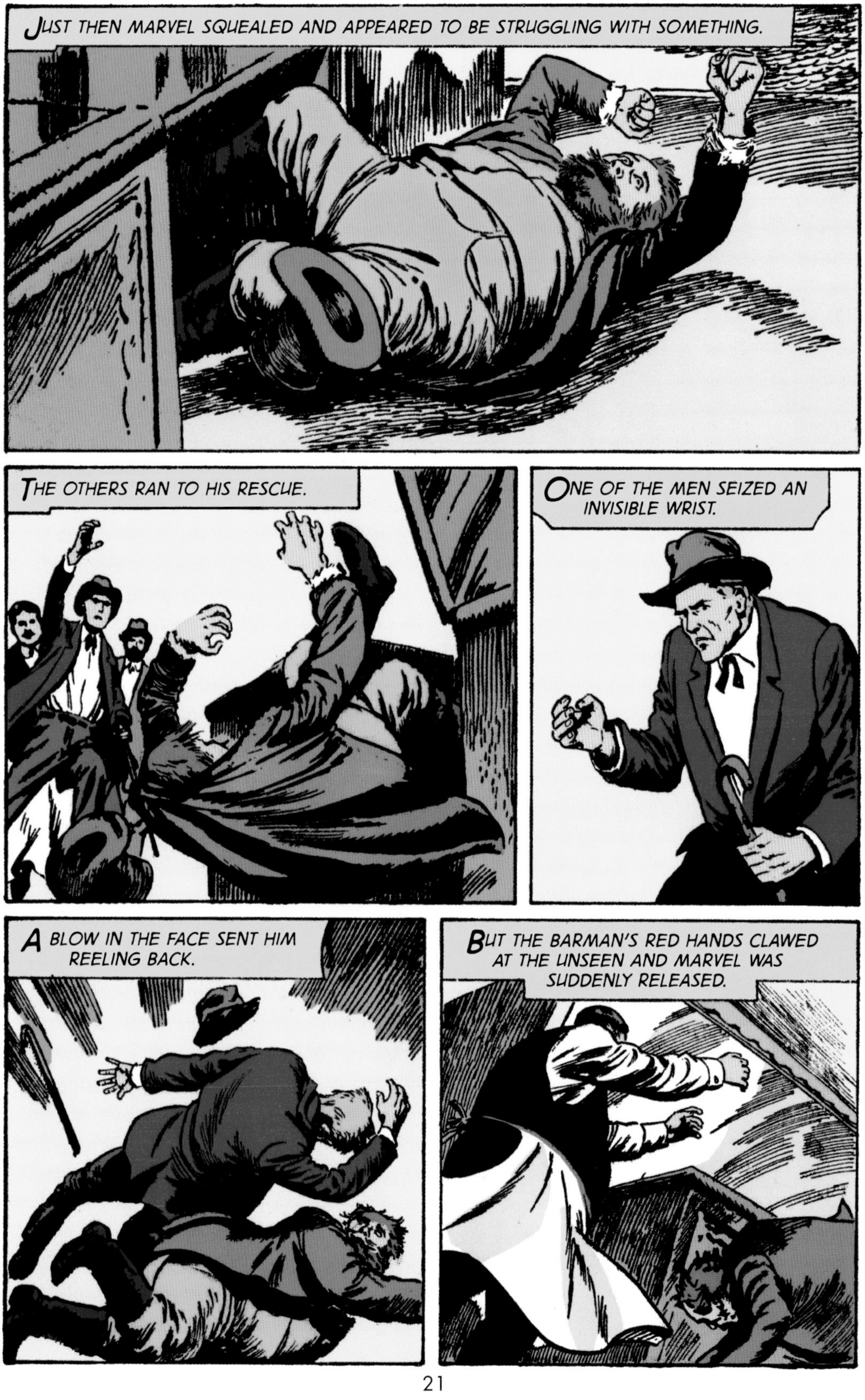
JUST THEN MARVEL SQUEALED AND APPEARED TO BE STRUGGLING WITH SOMETHING.
THE OTHERS RAN TO HIS RESCUE.
ONE OF THE MEN SEIZED AN INVISIBLE WRIST.
A BLOW IN THE FACE SENT HIM REELING BACK.
BUT THE BARMAN'S RED HANDS CLAWED AT THE UNSEEN AND MARVEL WAS SUDDENLY RELEASED.

THE FIGHT BLUNDERED AROUND THE DOOR.

THEN SUDDENLY, THE DOOR SLAMMED, AND THE MEN FOUND THEMSELVES STRUGGLING WITH EMPTY AIR.

WHERE'S HE GONE OUT?

THIS WAY I THINK.

I'LL SHOW HIM.

HE SWUNG HIS ARM IN A HORIZONTAL CURVE AND FIVE BULLETS RADIATED OUT INTO THE NARROW YARD.

COME ON, LET'S FEEL AROUND FOR THE BODY.

IN A HOUSE NEAR THE INN, A DOCTOR NAMED KEMP HEARD THE SHOTS.

WHO'S LETTING OFF REVOLVERS, I WONDER.

AN HOUR LATER HIS DOOR-BELL RANG, AND A SERVANT WENT TO ANSWER IT. WHEN SHE RETURNED...

WHO WAS THAT?

I DON'T KNOW, SIR. THERE WAS NO ONE THERE.

IT WAS TWO O'CLOCK BEFORE DOCTOR KEMP FINISHED HIS WORK FOT THE NIGHT. HE ROSE, YAWNED AND STARTED FOR BED.

WHEN HE REACHED HIS ROOM, HE SAW SOMETHING THAT ASTONISHED HIM.

THE DOOR-HANDLE IS BLOOD-STAINED!

He ENTERED THE ROOM AND HIS GLANCE FELL ON THE BED.

MORE BLOOD! AND THE SHEET IS TORN!

THEN HE HEARD A VOICE.

GOOD HEAVENS! IT'S KEMP!

SUDDENLY HE SAW A COILED AND BLOOD-STAINED BANDAGE HANGING IN MID-AIR.

He REACHED OUT TO TOUCH IT, AND THE VOICE CAME AGAIN.

KEEP YOUR NERVE, KEMP. I'M AN INVISIBLE MAN.

THIS IS NONSENSE! IT'S SOME TRICK.

HE REACHED AGAIN FOR THE BANDAGE, AND HIS HAND MET INVISIBLE FINGERS.

A FRANTIC DESIRE TO GET AWAY TOOK POSSESSION OF KEMP, BUT HE WAS TRIPPED AND FLUNG BACKWARDS ON THE BED.

HE OPENED HIS MOUTH TO SHOUT, AND THE CORNER OF THE SHEET WAS THRUST IN HIS TEETH.

STOP THAT, YOU FOOL! I'M REALLY AN INVISIBLE MAN. IT IS NO FOOLISHNESS AND NO MAGIC. I NEED YOUR HELP!

KEMP SAT UP QUIETLY.

I AM JUST AN ORDINARY MAN - ONE YOU HAVE KNOWN, IN FACT. I AM GRIFFIN, OF UNIVERSITY COLLEGE. I HAVE MADE MYSELF INVISIBLE.

I REMEMBER A STUDENT NAMED GRIFFIN, WHO WON THE MEDAL FOR CHEMISTRY. BUT I DON'T UNDERSTAND...

I'LL EXPLAIN LATER. BUT NOW I AM WOUNDED AND IN PAIN AND TIRED. I MUST REST.

HAVE YOU A DRESSING GOWN? THE NIGHT IS CHILLY TO A MAN WITHOUT CLOTHES.

KEMP HELD OUT A ROBE AND WATCHED AS IT FLUTTERED WEIRDLY IN THE AIR.

IN A MOMENT IT STOOD FULL AND DECOROUS,

HOW IN THE WORLD DID YOU GET LIKE THIS?

IT'S A PROCESS, SANE AND INTELLIGIBLE ENOUGH. I'LL TELL YOU TOMORROW. I MEANT TO KEEP IT TO MYSELF, BUT I MUST HAVE A PARTNER. WE CAN DO SUCH THINGS!

THE DRESSING GOWN ESCORTED KEMP OUT THE DOOR. IT CLOSED BEHIND HIM, AND KEMP HEARD THE KEY BEING TURNED IN THE LOCK.

AM I DREAMING? HAS THE WORLD GONE MAD – OR HAVE I?

THE FOLLOWING MORNING KEMP DESPATCHED A NOTE TO THE CHIEF OF POLICE. THEN HE AND THE INVISIBLE MAN SAT DOWN TO BREAKFAST.

BEFORE WE CAN DO ANYTHING, I MUST UNDERSTAND A LITTLE MORE ABOUT THIS INVISIBILITY OF YOURS.

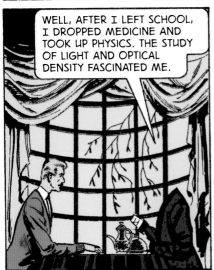

WELL, AFTER I LEFT SCHOOL, I DROPPED MEDICINE AND TOOK UP PHYSICS. THE STUDY OF LIGHT AND OPTICAL DENSITY FASCINATED ME.

AFTER MUCH STUDY I CAME UPON THE REALISATION THAT BONE AND FLESH AND HAIR AND NAILS - IN FACT, THE WHOLE FABRIC OF MAN EXCEPT THE RED IN HIS BLOOD - IS MADE UP OF COLOURLESS TRANSPARENT TISSUE.

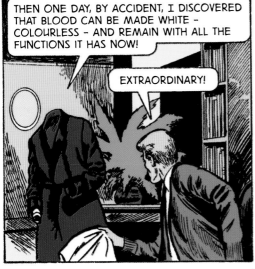

THEN ONE DAY, BY ACCIDENT, I DISCOVERED THAT BLOOD CAN BE MADE WHITE - COLOURLESS - AND REMAIN WITH ALL THE FUNCTIONS IT HAS NOW!

EXTRAORDINARY!

THEN I HAD AN OVERWHELMING THOUGHT. I COULD BE INVISIBLE!

"*I* WORKED THREE YEARS IN A RENTED ROOM IN LONDON BEFORE I FELT I HAD MASTERED THE PROCESS...

JUST THINK WHAT IT WOULD MEAN TO BE INVISIBLE! THE MYSTERY, THE POWER, THE FREEDOM!

"*ONE* NIGHT I TOOK THE DRUGS.

"*THE* PROCESS TOOK ALL NIGHT TO COMPLETE. BY MORNING I WAS INVISIBLE. I STOOD BEFORE THE MIRROR, AND SAW NOTHING.

"*TO* COVER MY TRAIL AND KEEP MY SECRET FROM FALLING INTO OTHER HANDS, I TOSSED TOGETHER SOME LOOSE PAPER AND STRAW AND LIT IT.

"*WITH* THE HOUSE FLAMING BEHIND ME, I SLIPPED OUT INTO THE STREET.

"HARDLY HAD I EMERGED WHEN I WAS HIT VIOLENTLY FROM BEHIND BY A MAN CARRYING A BASKET.

"HE LOOKED SO SURPRISED THAT I COULD NOT RESIST TWISTING IT FROM HIM AND SWINGING IT INTO THE AIR.

"THIS ATTRACTED THE ATTENTION OF THE PASSERS-BY. I DODGED BACK AND RAN UP THE STEPS OF A HOUSE.

"JUST THEN A COUPLE OF BOYS STOPPED AND BEGAN LOOKING CURIOUSLY AT THE STEPS.

SEE 'EM. MUDDY FOOTMARKS - BARE.

"I FLED AND THE BOYS STARED AT THE FOOTMARKS FLASHING DOWN THE STREET.

"I BEGAN TO REALISE THE FULL DISADVANTAGE OF MY CONDITION. I HAD NO SHELTER, NO COVERING. I WAS A VICTIM OF THE WEATHER AND ALL ITS CONSEQUENCES.

"I COULD NOT GO ABROAD IN SNOW. IT WOULD SETTLE ON ME AND EXPOSE ME. RAIN, TOO, WOULD MAKE ME A WATERY OUTLINE.

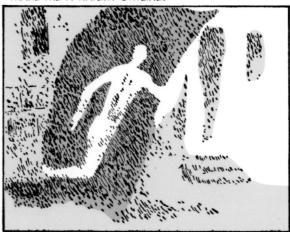

"I BEGAN TO GET DESPARATE, FOR I WAS HUNGRY AND VERY COLD. THEN I SAW A LITTLE SHOP NEAR DRURY LANE WHICH SOLD THEATRICAL COSTUMES.

"I SLIPPED IN AND HAD STARTED TO RUMMAGE AMONG THE OLD CLOTHES WHEN THE OWNER CAME IN.

IS THERE ANYONE THERE?

"I EDGED AWAY, AND A PLANK CREAKED. HE PULLED OUT A REVOLVER...

WHO'S THERE?

"WITH THAT I FLEW INTO A RAGE AND KNOCKED HIM ON THE HEAD.

"I GAGGED HIM AND TIED HIM UP IN A SHEET.

"THEN I DRESSED MYSELF IN SOME OF THE CLOTHES, AND CHOSE A MASK, DARK GLASSES, WHISKERS AND A WIG.

"I BROKE INTO HIS CUPBOARD AND TOOK SOME MONEY. FINALLY I WAS READY TO GO FORTH INTO THE WORLD AGAIN, FULLY EQUIPPED. SCREWING UP MY COURAGE, I MARCHED OUT INTO THE STREET.

"NO ONE NOTICED ME PARTICULARLY, AND I WENT INTO A PLACE TO ORDER LUNCH.

FOOL! YOU CANNOT EAT WITH THIS MASK ON!

"*I LEFT, AND SUBSTITUTED A BANDAGE FOR THE MASK. LATER I THOUGHT IT OVER. I REALISED WHAT A HELPLESS ABSURDITY AN INVISIBLE MAN WAS. WHAT WAS I TO DO? I HAD BECOME A WRAPPED UP MYSTERY, A BANDAGED CARICATURE OF A MAN.*"

THEN I WENT TO IPING, TO WORK ON A WAY OF GETTING BACK. WHEN I HAVE DONE ALL I MEAN TO DO INVISIBLY, I WANT TO BE ABLE TO BE VISIBLE AGAIN.

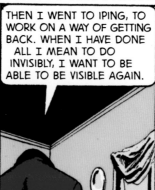

WERE YOU EVER TROUBLED ABOUT THE MAN YOU LEFT TIED UP IN A SHEET?

I SUPPOSE HE UNTIED HIMSELF. THE KNOTS WERE PRETTY TIGHT, THOUGH.

BY HEAVEN, KEMP, YOU DON'T KNOW WHAT RAGE IS! TO HAVE WORKED FOR YEARS, TO HAVE PLANNED AND PLOTTED, AND THEN TO GET SOME FUMBLING IDIOT MESSING ACROSS YOUR COURSE!

IF I HAVE MUCH MORE OF IT, I SHALL GO WILD – I SHALL START MOWING THEM DOWN!

BUT NOW, WHAT ARE YOU GOING TO DO?

I MUST HAVE A CONFEDERATE, A HELPER, AN ARRANGEMENT WHEREBY I CAN EAT AND SLEEP AND REST UNSUSPECTED.

ALONE I CAN ROB A LITTLE, HURT A LITTLE, BUT THERE IS THE END. BUT WITH A CONFEDERATE, I CAN ESTABLISH A REIGN OF TERROR. I WILL ISSUE ORDERS AND ALL WHO DISOBEY THEM I WILL KILL.

BUT WHY MUST YOU KILL?

TO TERRIFY AND DOMINATE. BUT HUSH, WHAT IS THAT NOISE DOWNSTAIRS?

NOTHING.

SOMEONE IS COMING UPSTAIRS! YOU HAVE BETRAYED ME!

SWIFTLY THE INVISIBLE MAN BEGAN TO TAKE OFF HIS ROBE.

KEMP FLUNG OPEN THE DOOR, DODGED OUT, AND SLAMMED IT IN THE INVISIBLE MAN'S FACE.

BUT WITH A WRENCH THE INVISIBLE MAN OPENED IT AND THREW KEMP BACKWARDS

HE DASHED DOWN THE STAIRS AND COLLIDED WITH COLONEL ADYE, THE CHIEF OF POLICE.

THE FRONT DOOR OPENED AND SHUT VIOLENTLY.

THE GAME'S UP! HE'S GONE!

KEMP TOLD HIS STORY TO THE COLONEL.

HE'S MAD - INHUMAN! HE THINKS OF NOTHING BUT HIS OWN SAFETY. HE HAS WOUNDED MEN; HE WILL KILL THEM UNLESS WE CAN PREVENT HIM. HE HAS GONE OUT NOW - FURIOUS!

HE MUST BE CAUGHT. THAT IS CERTAIN. BUT HOW?

ONCE HE GETS AWAY HE MAY GO THROUGH THE COUNTRYSIDE KILLING AND MAIMING. HE DREAMS OF A REIGN OF TERROR! WE MUST PREVENT HIM FROM LEAVING THE DISTRICT. WE MUST SET A WATCH ON TRAINS AND ROADS AND SHIPPING.

AND WE MUST KEEP HIM FROM EATING OR SLEEPING. ALL FOOD MUST BE LOCKED UP, AND HOUSES EVERYWHERE BARRED. THE WHOLE COUNTRYSIDE MUST BEGIN HUNTING AND KEEP HUNTING UNTIL HE IS SECURED. THE MAN HAS BECOME INHUMAN. IT IS FRIGHTFUL TO THINK OF WHAT HE MAY DO!

THE INVISIBLE MAN WAS NOT HEARD OF FOR SEVERAL HOURS, DURING WHICH TIME THE COUNTRYSIDE ORGANISED TO PREVENT HIS ESCAPE. THE FOLLOWING DAY KEMP RECEIVED A LETTER.

THIS ANNOUNCES THE FIRST DAY OF THE TERROR. THIS IS DAY ONE OF YEAR ONE OF THE EPOCH OF THE INVISIBLE MAN. I AM INVISIBLE MAN THE FIRST. THERE WILL BE ONE EXECUTION FOR THE SAKE OF EXAMPLE... A MAN NAMED KEMP. DEATH, THE UNSEEN DEATH, IS COMING. TODAY KEMP IS TO DIE!

KEMP RANG FOR HIS HOUSEKEEPER.

PLEASE GO AROUND THE HOUSE. MAKE SURE ALL THE WINDOWS ARE LOCKED, AND CLOSE THE SHUTTERS.

HE SWIFTLY WROTE A NOTE.

THEN TAKE THIS TO POLICE COLONEL ADYE.

YES, SIR.

HE STOOD AT THE WINDOW AND STARED OUT AT THE STILL COUNTRYSIDE.

HE'S OUT THERE. HE MAY BE WATCHING ME NOW.

BEFORE LONG THE DOORBELL RANG. IT WAS COLONEL ADYE.

HE'S CLOSE ABOUT HERE, KEMP. HE SNATCHED THAT NOTE OF YOURS FROM YOUR SERVANT'S HAND. SHE'S DOWN AT THE STATION-HOUSE NOW.

JUST THEN A RESOUNDING SMASH OF GLASS CAME FROM UPSTAIRS.

COME ON, LET'S SEE WHAT IT IS.

THEY FOUND TWO OF THE STUDY WINDOWS SHATTERED.

IS THERE A WAY OF CLIMBING UP HERE?

NO, NOT EVEN FOR A CAT.

THE SOUND OF MORE GLASS SHATTERING SENT THEM DOWNSTAIRS AGAIN.

HE MEANS TO BREAK EVERY WINDOW IN THE HOUSE. BUT HE'S A FOOL. THE WIDOWS DOWN HERE HAVE SHUTTERS. HE CAN'T GET IN.

I'LL GO DOWN TO THE STATION-HOUSE AND GET THE BLOODHOUNDS PUT ON HIM. THAT OUGHT TO SETTLE HIM!

ADYE SLIPPED OUT, AND KEMP BOLTED THE DOOR BEHIND HIM.

THEN, WATCHING FROM THE WINDOW, KEMP SAW THE POLICEMAN STOP SUDDENLY.

THERE WAS A LITTLE PUFF OF BLUE IN THE AIR AND ADYE FELL FORWARD.

THE INVISIBLE MAN WAS WAITING FOR HIM!

KEMP ARMED HIMSELF WITH A POKER AND WAITED...

SUDDENLY THE HOUSE RESOUNDED WITH HEAVY BLOWS AND THE SPLINTERING OF WOOD.

THE SHUTTERS ARE BEING DRIVEN IN WITH AN AXE! IN A MOMENT, HE WILL BE INSIDE!

KEMP RETREATED TO THE KITCHEN, LOCKING THE DOOR AFTER HIM.

THE DOORBELL RANG. KEMP CAUTIOUSLY ADMITTED TWO POLICEMEN.

THE INVISIBLE MAN! HE'S IN THE HOUSE, AND HE HAS AN AXE!

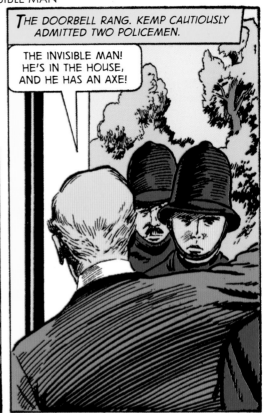

HERE, TAKE THESE POKERS.

SUDDENLY THE DOOR BURST OPEN, AND ONE OF THE POLICEMEN CAUGHT AN AXE BLOW ON HIS POKER.

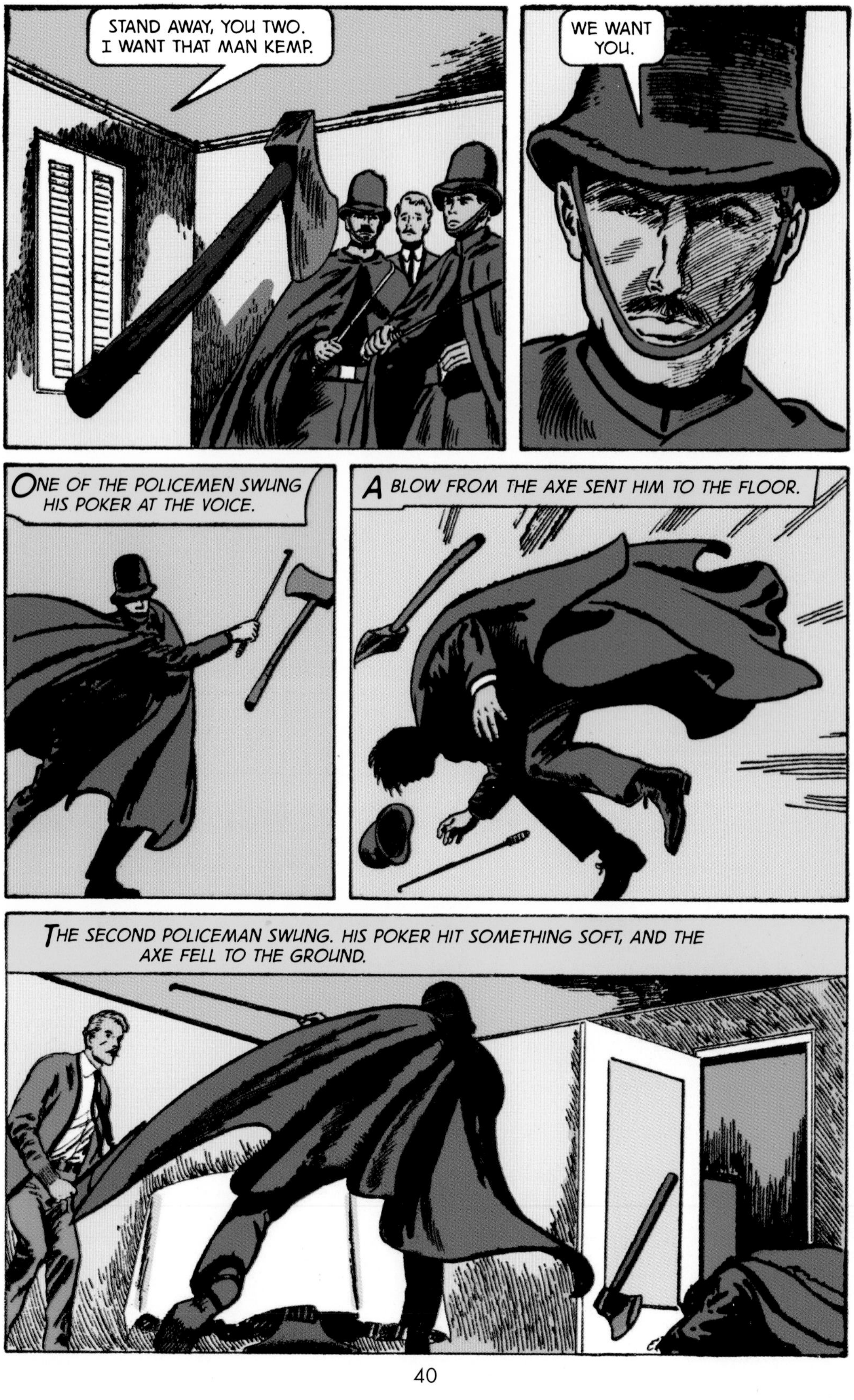
STAND AWAY, YOU TWO. I WANT THAT MAN KEMP.
WE WANT YOU.
ONE OF THE POLICEMEN SWUNG HIS POKER AT THE VOICE.
A BLOW FROM THE AXE SENT HIM TO THE FLOOR.
THE SECOND POLICEMAN SWUNG. HIS POKER HIT SOMETHING SOFT, AND THE AXE FELL TO THE GROUND.

KEMP FLUNG OPEN A WINDOW AND JUMPED OUT.

HE RAN AS FAST AS HE COULD TOWARDS THE TOWN.

AS HE SPED ALONG, HE HEARD FOOTSTEPS BEHIND HIM.

FINALLY HE REACHED A GROUP OF PEOPLE.

THE INVISIBLE MAN! HE'S AFTER ME!

WOMEN SCREAMED AND CHILDREN SCATTERED AS HE POUNDED PAST.

HE REACHED A KNOT OF MEN AND STOPPED.

HE'S CLOSE HERE! WE CAN CATCH HIM! FORM A LINE ACROSS –

SUDDENLY KEMP WAS HIT HARD.

AS HE SPRAWLED ON THE GROUND AN UNSEEN KNEE WENT INTO HIS DIAPHRAGM AND A PAIR OF EAGER HANDS GRIPPED HIS THROAT.

A MAN RAN UP AND SWUNG A SPADE THROUGH THE AIR ABOVE KEMP.

THERE WAS A DULL THUD, AND THE GRIP ON KEMP'S THROAT RELAXED.

WE'VE GOT HIM!

A NUMBER OF BURLY MEN RUSHED UP.

HE'S DOWN! HOLD HIS FEET!

THERE WAS A SAVAGE STRUGGLE.

THEN...

STAND BACK! HE'S HURT.

DON'T LET GO OF HIM! HE MAY BE SHAMMING.

NO, HE'S NOT SHAMMING.

HE'S NOT BREATHING, AND THERE'S NO HEARTBEAT. HE'S DEAD.

SUDDENLY AN OLD WOMAN SCREAMED AND THRUST OUT A WRINKLED FINGER.

LOOKY THERE! I CAN SEE HIS HAND!

HULLO! HERE'S HIS FEET A-SHOWING!

SLOWLY THE BRUISED AND BROKEN OUTLINE OF A BODY APPEARED. THE CROWD GAZED IN TENSE SILENCE AS THE INVISIBLE MAN BECAME ONCE AGAIN VISIBLE.

THEN SOMEONE BROUGHT A SHEET AND, HAVING COVERED HIM, THEY CARRIED HIM INTO A HOUSE.

THE END

NOW THAT YOU HAVE READ THE CLASSICS ILLUSTRATED EDITION, WHY NOT GO ON TO READ THE ORIGINAL VERSION TO GET THE FULL ENJOYMENT OF THIS CLASSIC WORK?

The Invisible Man - A Synopsis

The Invisible Man: A Grotesque Romance begins in England, on a wintry day in February. A mysterious, oddly dressed stranger arrives at the Coach and Horses inn, in the town of Iping in rural Sussex. The man's face is covered completely with bandages, and he wears a large hat, gloves and dark glasses. Although the landlady and her husband, the Halls, are curious about his bizarre appearance, they readily agree to rent him a room because it is the off season. The next day, the stranger's luggage arrives, consisting of several crates of chemicals and numerous books.

Local residents assume he is disfigured or burned and simply wants to hide his true appearance. He is reclusive and his only request is that he be left alone.

Soon after the arrival of the stranger, a series of mysterious thefts occur in the village. Local residents never see the thief and suspicion immediately falls on the new arrival.

One morning when the innkeepers pass the stranger's room, they enter, noticing the stranger's clothes scattered all over the floor, but the stranger himself is nowhere to be seen. The furniture seems to spring to life and the bedclothes and a chair leap into mid-air and push them out of the room. Later in the day Mrs Hall confronts their guest about this and he reveals that he is, in fact, invisible, removing his bandages and goggles to reveal nothing beneath. Mrs Hall flees in horror and a chase ensues. The police attempt to catch the stranger, but as he throws off all of his clothes, he becomes invisible and escapes.

The (now completely) Invisible Man flees to the downs, where he frightens a tramp, Thomas Marvel, with his invisibility and forces Marvel to become his assistant. They return to the village, where, as agreed, Marvel steals the Invisible Man's books and apparatus from the inn, while the Invisible Man himself steals clothes from the local doctor and vicar. Shortly after the theft, Marvel attempts to betray the Invisible Man to the police and the Invisible Man chases after him, threatening to kill him.

Marvel flees to the seaside town of Burdock where he takes refuge in an inn. Following closely behind, the Invisible Man attempts to break into the inn through the back door, but he is discovered and subsequently shot by a black-bearded American. The Invisible Man flees the scene, now badly injured. He enters a nearby house to take refuge and attend to his wound. The house belongs to one Dr Kemp, whom the Invisible Man recognises immediately. He reveals to Kemp his true identity - Griffin, a brilliant medical student with whom Kemp studied at university.

Griffin explains to Kemp that after leaving university he was desperately poor. Determined to achieve something of scientific significance, he began work on an experiment to make people and objects invisible. To fund his research he used money stolen from his own father, who committed suicide after being robbed by his son.

Griffin experimented with a formula that altered the refractive index of objects, which resulted in light not bending when passing through the object, thereby making it invisible. He performed the experiment **Cont'd** on a cat, but when the cat's owner, Griffin's neighbour, realised her cat was missing, she made a complaint to their landlord, and Griffin was forced to use the invisibility formula on himself to hide. Griffin theorises that part of the reason he can be invisible stems from the fact he is albino, mentioning also that food becomes visible in his stomach and remains so until digested, with the bizarre image passing through air in the meantime.

After burning the boarding house down to cover his tracks, he began to feel a sense of invincibility growing from being invisible. However, reality soon proved that sense more than somewhat misguided. After struggling to survive out in the open, he stole some clothing from a tawdry backstreet shop and took residence at the Coach & Horses inn to reverse the experiment.

He then explains to Kemp that he now plans to begin a reign of terror, using his invisibility to terrorise the nation, and with Kemp acting as his secret confederate.

Realising that Griffin is clearly insane, Kemp decides to alert the police. When the police arrive, Griffin, feeling betrayed, violently assaults both Kemp and a policeman before escaping.

The next day he leaves a note on Kemp's doorstep announcing that Kemp will be the first man killed in the reign of terror. Kemp remains calm and writes a note to the Colonel, detailing a plan to use himself as bait to trap the Invisible Man, but as a maidservant attempts to deliver the note she is attacked by Griffin and the note is stolen.

Just as the police accompany the attacked maid back to Kemp's house, the Invisible Man breaks in through the back door and makes for Kemp. Kemp dashes from the house and runs down the hill to the town below, where he alerts a workman that the Invisible Man is approaching.

The people of the town, witnessing the pursuit, rally around Kemp. When Kemp is pinned down by Griffin, the workman strikes him with a spade and knocks him to the ground, where he is violently assaulted by the crowd. Kemp calls for the mob to stop, but he is too late.

The Invisible Man dies of the injuries he has received, and his naked and battered body slowly becomes visible on the ground.

Later it is revealed that Marvel has Griffin's notes, with the invisibility formula written in a mix of Russian and Greek which Marvel cannot read, and with some pages washed out, leaving the formula unintelligible to all.

Notable Events of 1897

1897

- **March 4th** - William McKinley succeeds Grover Cleveland as President of the United States.

- **April 3rd** - Johannes Brahms, German composer, dies.

- **May 18th** - Bram Stoker's novel *Dracula* goes on sale in London.

- **May 19th** - Oscar Wilde is released from Reading Gaol.

- **June 2nd** - Mark Twain, responding to rumours that he was dead, is quoted by the New York Journal as saying, "The report of my death was an exaggeration."

- **June 22nd** - Queen Victoria celebrates her Diamond Jubilee.

- **July 25th** - Writer Jack London sails to join the Klondike Gold Rush where he will write his first successful stories.

- **August 11th** - Enid Blyton, British children's writer, is born.

- **August 31st** - Thomas Edison patents the Kinetoscope - the first movie projector.

- **September 25th** - William Faulkner, American writer, Nobel Prize laureate, is born.

- **December 28th** - The play *Cyrano de Bergerac*, by Edmond Rostand, premieres in Paris.

- **(undated)** - The word "computer", meaning an electronic calculation device, is first used.

Notable Films Taken from the Works of H. G. Wells

1902 - *A Trip to the Moon* (the world's first science fiction film, based loosely on Jules Verne's *From the Earth to the Moon* and H. G. Wells' *The First Men in the Moon*)

1919 - *The First Men in the Moon*

1933 - *The Invisible Man*

1933 - *Island of Lost Souls* (based on Wells' 1896 novel *The Island of Dr Moreau*)

1936 - *Things to Come* (Wells wrote the screenplay based loosely on his 1933 novel *The Shape of Things to Come* and his 1931 non-fiction work, *The Work, Wealth and Happiness of Mankind*)

1953 - *The War of the Worlds* (the first screen adaptation of Wells' seminal work)

1960 - *The Time Machine*

1964 - *First Men in the Moon*

1977 - *The Island of Dr Moreau*

1977 - *Empire of the Ants* (based very loosely on Wells' 1905 short story of the same name)

2002 - *The Time Machine* (directed by Simon Wells - the great-grandson of H. G. Wells)

2005 - *War of the Worlds* (Steven Spielberg's epic production of Wells' work starring Tom Cruise)

2007 - *The History of Mr Polly* (a UK television version starring Lee Evans as Mr Polly)